Deck the Halls

A Canadian Christmas Carol

Deck the Halls

A Canadian Christmas Carol

Helaine Becker

illustrated by
Werner Zimmermann

North Winds Press
An Imprint of Scholastic Canada Ltd.

The paintings for this book were created in pencil, ink and watercolour on Arches 90 lb hot press paper.

Library and Archives Canada Cataloguing in Publication

Becker, Helaine, 1961-, author
Deck the halls : a Canadian Christmas carol / Helaine Becker;
illustrated by Werner Zimmermann.

ISBN 978-1-4431-4836-8 (hardback)

1. Christmas--Juvenile poetry. 2. Canada--Juvenile poetry.
I. Zimmermann, H. Werner (Heinz Werner), 1951-, illustrator
II. Title.

PS8553.E295532D43 2016   jC811'.6   C2016-902219-6

www.scholastic.ca

6 5 4 3 2 1   Printed in Canada 114   16 17 18 19 20

Still for Karl.
🌿 H.B.

To Little Ava V.
🌿 W.Z.

Deck the halls with boughs of holly,
Fa-la-la-la-la, la-la-la-la.
Porcupine is feeling jolly!
Fa-la-la-la-la, la-la-la-la.

Beavers building, busy, busy,
Fa-la-la, la-la-la, la-la-la.

Loons try toe loops and get dizzy!
Fa-la-la-la-la, la-la-la-la.

Don we now our reindeer sweaters,
Fa-la-la-la-la, la-la-la-la.

Muskox like their own coats better!
Fa-la-la-la-la, la-la-la-la.

Caribou in pompom hoodies,
Fa-la-la, la-la-la, la-la-la.

Raid the groaning board of goodies,
Fa-la-la-la-la, la-la-la-la.

Bear cubs gather logs and kindling,
Fa-la-la-la-la, la-la-la-la.

Keep the yule log flames from dwindling,
Fa-la-la-la-la, la-la-la-la.

Round the tree the dogs are racing,
Fa-la-la, la-la-la, la-la-la.

Right behind, raccoons are chasing!
Fa-la-la-la-la, la-la-la-la.

'Neath the tree are presents, heaping,
Fa-la-la-la-la, la-la-la-la.

Hockey players are a-leaping,
Fa-la-la-la-la, la-la-la-la.

Otters carol, a cappella,
Fa-la-la, la-la-la, la-la-la.

Polar bear's one happy fella!
Fa-la-la-la-la, la-la-la-la.

In the armchair, look who's napping,
Fa-la-la-la-la, la-la-la-la.

Sasquatch is all thumbs at wrapping!
Fa-la-la-la-la, la-la-la-la.

Squirrels curled up by the fire,
Fa-la-la, la-la-la, la-la-la.

Lulled to sleep by
the moose choir!
Fa-la-la-la-la,
la-la-la-la.

Drifting into
dream-filled sleep,
Fa-la-la-la-la, la-la-la-la.
Christmas magic, yours to keep,
Fa-la-la-la-la, la-la-la-la.

So deck the halls
with boughs of holly,
Fa-la-la, la-la-la, la-la-la.

Make your True North
Christmas jolly!
Fa-la-la-la-la, la-la-la-la!

Deck the Halls

Traditional Christmas carol